THE HOUSE THAT JACK BUILT

illustrated by

Rodney Peppé

DELACORTE PRESS/NEW YORK

For Christen

Published by
Delacorte Press
1 Dag Hammarskjold Plaza
New York, N.Y. 10017

Originally published in England by Longman Group Ltd.

Manufactured in the United States of America

New Delacorte Edition—May 1985

Library of Congress Cataloging in Publication Data

The Library of Congress has cataloged the first
printing of this title as follows:
The house that Jack built.
    The house that Jack built.   Illustrated by Rodney Peppé.
  1st American ed.   New York, Delacorte Press [1970]
      32 p.   col. illus.   19 x 25 cm.   3.95
    A cumulative nursery rhyme about the chain of events that started
  when Jack built a house.
[1. Nursery rhymes]   I. Peppé, Rodney, illus.   II. Title.
PZ8.3.H79Pe 3   398.8   78-112054
ISBN 0-385-28430-6   MARC
Library of Congress   70 [4]   AC

This is the house . . .

. . . that Jack built.

This is the malt

That lay in the house
that Jack built.

This is the rat,
That ate the malt

That lay in the house that Jack built.

This is the cat,
That killed the rat,
That ate the malt
That lay in the house
that Jack built.

This is the dog,

That worried the cat,
That killed the rat,
That ate the malt
That lay in the house
that Jack built.

This is the cow with the crumpled horn,

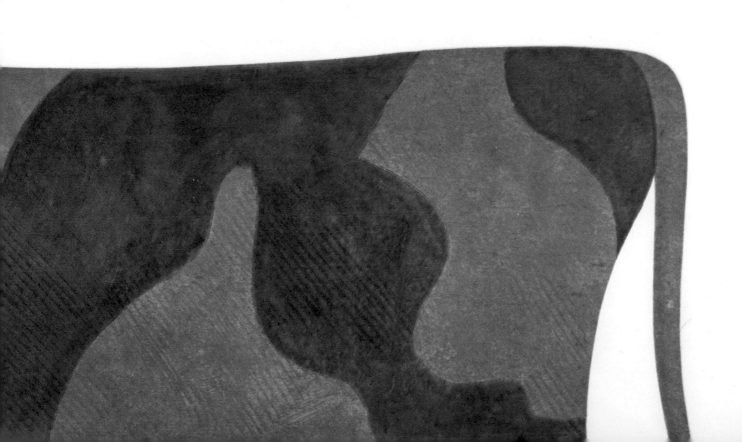

That tossed the dog,
That worried the cat,
That killed the rat,

That ate the malt
That lay in the house
that Jack built.

This is the maiden all forlorn,
That milked the cow
with the crumpled horn,
That tossed the dog,
That worried the cat,
That killed the rat,
That ate the malt
That lay in the
house that
Jack built.

This is the man all tattered and torn,

That kissed the maiden all forlorn,
That milked the cow with the crumpled horn,
That tossed the dog,
That worried the cat,
That killed the rat,
That ate the malt
That lay in the house that Jack built.

This is the priest
all shaven and shorn,

That married the man all tattered and torn,
That kissed the maiden all forlorn,
That milked the cow with the crumpled horn,
That tossed the dog,
That worried the cat,
That killed the rat,
That ate the malt
That lay in the house
that Jack built.

This is the cock  that crowed in the morn,

That waked the priest all shaven and shorn,
That married the man all tattered and torn,
That kissed the maiden all forlorn,
That milked the cow with the crumpled horn,
That tossed the dog,
That worried the cat,
That killed the rat,
That ate the malt
That lay in the house
that Jack built.

This is the farmer sowing his corn,

That kept the cock . . .

That waked
the priest . . .

That married
the man . . .

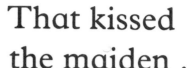

That kissed
the maiden . . .

That milked the cow . . .   That tossed the dog,

That worried the cat,

That killed the rat,

That lay in the house . . .

That ate the malt

. . . that Jack built.